59372088933935    FTBC

D0603515

WITHDRAWN
WORN, SOILED, OBSOLETE

# BEASTLY
## BABIES

words by

ELLEN JACKSON

beasts by

BRENDAN WENZEL

beach lane books

new york   london   toronto   sydney   new delhi

 **BEACH LANE BOOKS** • An imprint of Simon & Schuster Children's Publishing Division • 1230 Avenue of the Americas, New York, New York 10020 • Text copyright © 2015 by Ellen Jackson • Illustrations copyright © 2015 by Brendan Wenzel • All rights reserved, including the right of reproduction in whole or in part in any form. • Beach Lane Books is a trademark of Simon & Schuster, Inc. • For information about special discounts for bulk purchases, please contact Simon & Schuster Special Sales at 1-866-506-1949 or business@simonandschuster.com. • The Simon & Schuster Speakers Bureau can bring authors to your live event. For more information or to book an event, contact the Simon & Schuster Speakers Bureau at 1-866-248-3049 or visit our website at www.simonspeakers.com. • Book design by Lauren Rille • The text for this book is set in Zalderdash. • The illustrations for this book are rendered in almost everything imaginable. • Manufactured in China • 0415 SCP • First Edition • 10 9 8 7 6 5 4 3 2 1 • Jackson, Ellen, 1943– • Beastly babies / by Ellen Jackson ; illustrated by Brendan Wenzel. —First edition. • p. cm. • Summary: "Introduces all sorts of mischievous baby animals—and the grown-ups who love them no matter what"— Provided by publisher. • ISBN 978-1-4424-0834-0 (hardcover) • ISBN 978-1-4814-2585-8 (eBook) • [1. Stories in rhyme. 2. Animals—Infancy—Fiction.] I. Wenzel, Brendan, illustrator. II. Title. • PZ8.3.J1346Be 2015 • [E]—dc23 • 2014009702

To all the Beastly Babies I've known and loved,
especially Robin, Smokey, Daphne, Bailey, and Abby
—E.J.

To Nick, Lilah, and Adam,
you fantastic little beasts
—B.W.

Babies can be smooth
or hairy,

quail

or whale

or dromedary.

Babies can be one

or many,

lots and lots

or hardly any.

Mama tigers crawl and creep,
walking, stalking—then they leap.

Tiger babies pounce and fail
when they aim for Mama's tail.

Beaver mamas chomp and gnaw,
using teeth just like a saw.

Now the baby does it too,
biting more than he can chew!

Elephants of jumbo size
drowse and doze and close their eyes.

Babies butt and ram and slap—
there goes Mama's noontime nap!

Mama robin brings a treat,
slugs or bugs or something sweet.

Baby twitters, "Give me more!
I got three, but she got four!"

Baby rhino gets a nuzzle
from his mama's mega muzzle.

Munching, crunching, he'll grow large.
Watch him practice how to charge!

Mamas gather, weave, and shred
grass and leaves to make a bed.

Whether kit or chick or pup,
wriggling babies mess it up.

Puppies slobber,

kittens spill.

Young gorillas can't sit still.

Mamas gobble, mamas cluck.
Barnyard babies run amok!

Baby piglets will not wallow.
Baby ducklings do not follow.

Baby otters splash and splish.
Baby bear can't catch a fish.

Baby buffalo get grumpy.
Baby kangaroos get jumpy.

Baby octopi squirt ink.
Baby skunks cause quite a stink.

Making mischief,
having fun,
each is precious,
every one.

In a knoll, a hole,
or nest,
mamas love
*their* babies best.

Babies muss and fuss and cry—
but they grow up, by and by.

And what awaits them
when they're grown?

Beastly babies
of their own!